OH NO, School!

Published by
MAGINATION PRESS
An Educational Publishing Foundation Book
American Psychological Association
750 First Street NE
Washington, DC 20002

For more information about our books, including a complete catalog, please write to us,
call 1-800-374-2721, or visit our website at www.apa.org/pubs/magination.

Printed by Worzalla, Stevens Point, WI

Library of Congress Cataloging-in-Publication Data
Chang, Hae-Kyung.
[I hate going to kindergarten! English]
Oh no, school! / by Hae-Kyung Chang ; illustrated by Josee Bisaillon. — English edition.
pages cm
"An Educational Publishing Foundation Book."
Summary: With a stomp of her foot and tears in her eyes, Holly declares that she does not want
to go to school but her mother, aided by a favorite puppet, helps Holly find ways to solve her
kindergarten problems.
ISBN 978-1-4338-1333-7 (hardcover) — ISBN 1-4338-1333-5 (hardcover) — ISBN 978-1-4338-1334-4 (pbk.)
— ISBN 1-4338-1334-3 (pbk.) [1. Kindergarten—Fiction. 2. Schools—Fiction. 3. Mothers and daughters—
Fiction.] I. Bisaillon, Josée, illustrator. II. Title.
PZ7.C3596639Iah 2014
[E]—dc23
2013004873

OH NO, School!

by Hae-Kyung Chang

illustrated by Josée Bisaillon

MAGINATION PRESS • WASHINGTON, DC
American Psychological Association

This English edition is published by arrangement with EenBook Co., through the ChoiceMaker Korea Co.

One morning, Holly banged and stomped her feet, and her eyes filled up with tears.

"I don't want to go to school," she wailed.

Mommy was surprised.
"Holly, why don't you
want to go to school?"
she asked.

Holly sniffled, "Jenny keeps on...Robbie won't stop...Olivia doesn't listen..."

Mommy was busy putting her work clothes on.

Holly's face turned red. She started crying again and ran out of the room.

Mommy went to look for Holly.
She looked everywhere!

"Holly, come out!" said Mommy.

Mommy saw something sticking out
of the closet door in Holly's room.

Holly was sitting with her head down when the door creaked open.

Somebody tapped her on the shoulder.

"Hi, Holly. It's me, Bunny. I've looked everywhere for you."

"I know it's you, Mommy," said Holly.

"No, no. It's really me! Look!"

Holly looked up and saw Bunny, her favorite puppet.

Bunny tickled Holly and she began to smile a little.
"Heeheehee, hahaha! That tickles!" Holly burst into giggles.

"Is school that bad?" asked Bunny.

"Yes," said Holly.

"Can I try to guess why you don't want to go?" said Bunny.

"You can try," said Holly.

"Is it because...your friends keep taking your toys?"

"How did you know?" said Holly.

Bunny shrugged. "I guess it's because you and your friends like the same toys. Maybe next time, if someone tries to take the toy you chose, ask them if they want to play together. If you were a bunny like me, you might just hop away or hide the toy in the garden. But kids can share or take turns."

"There's something else," said Holly.

"Is Ms. Leonard's voice loud as thunder?" said Bunny.

"How did you know?" said Holly. "Her voice is so loud,
I'm scared."

"Ms. Leonard must speak loudly so everyone can
hear her," said Bunny. "She isn't angry. She just wants
you to learn your lessons. If kids had long rabbit ears
like me, she could talk very quietly."

"There's something else," said Holly.

"Do you have to practice your ABCs or sing or jump rope even if you're not sure how?" asked Bunny.

"Yes! Ms. Leonard tells me to sing even when I don't know the words," said Holly. "And we have to sit on the carpet with our legs crossed during story time."

"Doing something for the first time is hard," said Bunny. "You might feel embarrassed because you don't think you did it well. But if you keep trying and practicing then you will get better. Bunnies can sniff out carrots and lettuce, but only after they have practiced! You just have to try, and I will be very proud of you."

"Oh, Bunny!" Holly grabbed Bunny in a squishy hug.

Bunny and Mommy gave Holly a big hug back.

"Holly, I love you," said Mommy.

"I love you, too, Mommy!" said Holly.

Beep! Beep!

"Mommy, the school bus is here!"
said Holly. "I want to go to school!"

Holly jumped out of the closet.
"Bye, Mommy. Bye, Bunny!"
Holly waved and ran to catch the bus.

Mommy waved until Holly's bus
went around the corner.

"Oh no! I'm late!" Mommy said.
She forgot that she still had Bunny
on her hand as she rushed to work.

It looks like Bunny will spend the day
in Mommy's office today.

Sometimes you might not want to go to school.
Write or draw your reasons here:

Now, pretend your parents are Bunny. What do you think
they would say to help you feel better about going to school?
Write or draw what they might say here:

What do you like the best about going to school?
Draw or write about your fun and exciting school day here:

Note to Parents and Other Caregivers

by Elizabeth McCallum, PhD

Many young children experience difficulties when transitioning from home to school. These difficulties can manifest in a variety of ways, including behavior problems that occur in the home on school mornings or upon separation from parents when children are dropped off in the classroom. While these difficulties can be frustrating for parents and teachers, most often, they are within normal developmental limits and will subside with time as the child grows more confident in the school routine. However, there are steps parents and teachers can take to help children transition to school more easily.

HOW THIS BOOK CAN HELP

Oh No, School! is a delightful story about a young girl named Holly who does not want to go to kindergarten one morning. She screams, cries, and then hides in her closet when it is time to leave for the bus. Holly's mother employs Holly's favorite toy puppet to get to the bottom of Holly's reluctance to go to school. Soon Holly is racing off to meet the bus.

Most parents of young children have experienced some type of transitioning challenge relating to school. Reading this book with your child can be a fun and interactive way to discuss the issue of transitioning to school without speaking specifically about your child's own behavior. By discussing Holly's fears of school, children may be encouraged to engage in conversation about their own school-related concerns. After reading the book, you may wish to ask your child if she notices any of Holly's behaviors or statements that are similar to her own. This may help you to identify and address specific factors that are contributing to your child's anxiety about going to school.

COPING WITH NORMAL CHILDHOOD SCHOOL-RELATED ANXIETY

Young children resist going to school in a variety of ways and for a variety of reasons. Some children are anxious about leaving their parents; some are concerned about their ability to meet teacher expectations; and still others are simply tired and have trouble getting out of bed in the mornings. While this resistance can be exasperating for parents, it is most often a normal part of child development that will pass as your child becomes more comfortable in his or her school environment and routine. In the meantime, there are steps you can take to reduce your child's discomfort with school. The following guidelines may help your child transition to school more easily.

1. Help your child get accustomed to new school routines.
   Transition issues often arise upon the start of a new school year. Children can be anxious or fearful of actual or anticipated classroom experiences. You can help your child ease into a new school year by taking her to visit the classroom and meet the teacher before the school year

starts. It may also be helpful to obtain a schedule of routine activities from your child's teacher and share it with your child.

2. **Be clear about what your child can expect at school.**
Being open and honest about school routines and classroom rules will help your child cope with his school-related fears by reducing the likelihood of unanticipated classroom events. Many anxiety-related behavior problems are a result of fear of the unknown. When your child knows what to expect during the school day, he is less likely to exhibit these behaviors.

3. **Encourage your child to discuss concerns and fears about school.**
You should acknowledge your child's school-related fears and reassure her to the greatest extent possible. Some children become anxious upon being dropped off at school because they are fearful that their parents will not return to pick them up. You can reassure your child that you will be back and review the class routine so she is clear about when to expect your return.

4. **Enlist the school's help in reducing your child's discomfort.**
Identify a specific teacher or staff member who will help monitor your child's transition difficulties and be on board with any behavioral plan you may implement. This person should be knowledgeable of your child's preferred activities and areas of interest and be able to redirect your child toward them if he is experiencing difficulties.

5. **Use positive reinforcement for appropriate behavior.**
Deliver praise or small rewards contingent upon appropriate behavior. If your child has a particularly easy transition to school one morning, acknowledge and praise her for it. Remember to be specific about what behaviors in particular you are happy with. It may be helpful to employ a sticker chart system to reward your child for positive transition-related behaviors. Particularly with young children, minimal effort on your part in using positive reinforcement can go a long way towards increasing appropriate behavior.

6. **Set realistic expectations for behavior.**
Try to match your expectations for your child's behavior to his developmental level. Remember that all children (and adults for that matter) wake up on the wrong side of the bed some days, and some transition problems are to be expected. When these minor behavioral problems arise, the best method may be to simply ignore the behaviors and redirect the child to alternate activities or topics.

Discomfort or anxiety about going to school is common in young children and can occur for a variety of reasons. Most often, these difficulties will decrease as children become accustomed to their teachers and classroom routines. However, if your child's difficulties persist, or if they seem to cause particular emotional distress, it may be helpful to seek consultation from a licensed psychologist or psychotherapist.

Elizabeth McCallum, PhD, is an associate professor in the school psychology program at Duquesne University, as well as a Pennsylvania certified school psychologist. She is the author of many scholarly journal articles and book chapters on topics including academic and behavioral interventions for children and adolescents.

About the Author

Hae-Kyung Chang majored in child development psychology. Currently she works on children's educational programs and writes picture books. Her works include *The Cracking Date* and *The Moving Store*. She has also translated stories such as *Minerva the Monster, Poddy and Flora,* and *Mr. Big*.

About the Illustrator

Josée Bisaillon is an artist and illustrator from Canada. After drawing the characters on paper, she cuts them out and makes a collage, colors them again, and composes them on the computer to create rich images. She is the recipient of many awards for her use of various textures, bright colors, and her colorful imagination. She is the illustrator of *My Diary: The Totally True Story of ME!*, also published by Magination Press.

About Magination Press

Magination Press is an imprint of the American Psychological Association, the largest scientific and professional organization representing psychologists in the United States and the largest association of psychologists worldwide.